Latkes and Applesauce

A Hanukkah Story

by FRAN MANUSHKIN

Illustrated by ROBIN SPOWART

SCHOLASTIC INC. • *New York*

Copyright © 1990 by Fran Manushkin.

Illustrations copyright © 1990 by Robin Spowart.

All rights reserved. Published by Scholastic Inc.

SCHOLASTIC HARDCOVER is a registered trademark
of Scholastic Inc.

Library of Congress Cataloging-in-Publication Data
Manushkin, Fran.
Latkes and applesauce / by Fran Manushkin :
illustrated by Robin Spowart.
p. cm.
Summary: When a blizzard leaves a family housebound one Hanukkah,
they share what little food they have with some starving animals who
later return the favor.
ISBN 0-590-42261-8
[1. Hanukkah–Fiction.] I. Spowart, Robin, ill. II. Title.
PZ7.M3195Lat 1989

[E]—dc19   88-38916
                                                                  CIP

12 11 10 9 8 7 6 5 4 3 2 1   0 1 2 3 4 5/9

Printed in the U.S.A.   36

First Scholastic printing, October 1990

Design by Claire Counihan

For my favorite latke lovers,
Esther, Walter, Debbie,
and David Hautzig
— F.M.

To Rabbi David Kopstein
and Patti Philo
— R.S.

O you like to eat latkes and applesauce on Hanukkah? Of course you do. Who but a fool would say no to such a question! Well, here is a story about latkes and applesauce, and perhaps a miracle. Maybe yes, maybe no.

It happened long ago in a village far away, where there lived a little family named Menashe. Papa and Mama Menashe were tailors who had two children, Rebecca and Ezra.

Rebecca and Ezra were wonderful children who helped their mama and papa. Every year when it came time to celebrate Hanukkah, they dug up potatoes to make the latkes, and they picked the apples for applesauce.

But one year, winter came suddenly and snow began to fall — not just a lazy flake or two or a little bit of a flurry. No! This was a tremendous blizzard — as if all heaven's featherbeds had burst!

And when did this furious blizzard begin? Of course—on the first night of Hanukkah!

"Come, sunset is upon us," Papa called to his family. "It's time to light the candles and celebrate the Hanukkah miracle." So Papa sang the blessings and Mama lit the *shammes*, and Rebecca lit the first candle.

"Ah!" they sighed together at the beautiful light. Then Papa set the Hanukkah menorah in the window so all could see its glory.

"Now," declared Papa, "for the next eight days we shall celebrate the miracle of Hanukkah with feasting and gladness. Bring on the latkes and applesauce!"

"Papa," said Mama, "the blizzard has swallowed our feast. All of the potatoes are buried in the snow, and as for apples, this year we had so few."

"No latkes?" gasped Papa, and his bright eyes dimmed. "Ah well, then let us sip our soup."

So, sitting as closely as birds in a nest, Mama and Papa and Rebecca and Ezra sipped their soup together. Then they sang a joyful Hanukkah song with the wind whistling along through the walls.

"Sssh!" said Rebecca, suddenly. "I hear someone crying."
Soon they all heard it—a mewing and crying—as if all the sad
spirits in the world were set loose! Rebecca opened the door
a crack, and in walked a wet orange kitten!

"Mew, mew, mew!" the kitten cried.

Rebecca quickly patted her dry with a rag. "Papa," said Rebecca, "the kitten must have seen our candles!"

Mama filled a tiny dish with milk. After the kitten lapped it up, she purred, falling asleep in Rebecca's lap.

"Now, Rebecca," said Papa firmly, "we must return this kitten to her mother."

Rebecca shook her head. "Papa, this kitten hasn't *got* a mother. No mother would let her kitten wander alone in a storm!"

"Yes," agreed Ezra. "That is why the kitten was crying. And since you said we mustn't be sad on Hanukkah, I think we should keep this kitten."

"Sad? A cat?" Papa pulled at his beard.

"A cat is one of God's creatures," declared Mama. "Of course we will care for her."

Rebecca leaped up and hugged her mother. "Mama, what shall we name her?"

"A name should fit as well as a glove," said Papa. "Take care to name her well."

"I will," Rebecca promised, "but right now I want to play dreidel."

The little kitten spun the dreidel so well, she won two nuts and a raisin! And when the candles flickered out, everyone went to bed.

On the second night of Hanukkah, the snow came down even harder! Again Mama lit the candles, and Papa placed the Hanukkah menorah in the window, and again the family sat down to their soup.

"I'm not complaining," Papa said to Mama. "I like soup as much as you, but I'd love to wrap my mouth around a latke!"

"Miracles have happened before," answered Mama. "Remember, two thousand years ago—"

"*Shush!*" interrupted Papa. "Did you hear that noise?" It was a shrill bark—right outside the door. Ezra leaped up and opened the door a crack—and in walked a skinny brown dog.

"This dog looks hungry as a bear!" said Ezra. He scooped the last drumstick from his soup, and the dog quickly gobbled it up.

"Ezra," praised Papa, "you are a generous boy. But you know we cannot keep this dog. We have hardly enough to feed ourselves!"

"But Papa," said Rebecca. "This dog is *starving*. Haven't you said we must feast on Hanukkah?"

"Feasting? A dog?" Papa pulled at his beard. "Ah well, a dog is one of God's creatures too. Let him stay and share what we have."

Ezra leaped up and gave Papa a hug. "I will think of a good name for our dog," Ezra promised. "A name should fit as well as a glove."

That night, the dog played dreidel with the kitten. And when the candles flickered out, everyone went to bed.

On the third night of Hanukkah, the snow was still falling. Mama sighed, "Our soup is dwindling like a burning
candle. If the snow doesn't stop, we'll surely starve!"

"Now, now," said Papa sagely. "Where there's life,
there's hope." On the fourth night, as the snow kept falling,
Papa repeated these words. As he did on the fifth night,
when bread was all they ate. And on the sixth and seventh,
when crumbs were all they had.

On the eighth night, after Mama lit the last candle, Papa said, "I see the sky is beginning to clear. Let us go out and gaze at the stars. Perhaps they can help us forget our empty stomachs."

So everyone piled on their sweaters and pants and socks. The kitten and the dog already had their own coats, so they rushed out ahead.

The dog leaped around in the moonlit snow. He leaped and ran and sniffed and dug.

"Papa?" asked Ezra. "Why is our dog digging?"

"It is in a dog's nature to dig," said Papa, stepping closer to admire the dog's work.

All of a sudden, Papa gasped. "Oh, what a world of
wonders this is! Our dog has dug up potatoes!"

"Potatoes in the snow?" shouted Mama. "It's a miracle!"

"We will have latkes tonight!" shouted Papa.

"*Mew, mew, mew,*" came a cry from above. Papa gazed up at the heavens. "The Holy One doesn't mew," said Papa, "so our kitten must have climbed up this tree."

"Why is she crying?" Rebecca asked.

Papa answered sagely, "It is in a kitten's nature to climb and cry to come down, and it is in a person's nature to help her." Quickly, Papa tucked his sweater into his pants and began climbing up the tree.

After slipping and struggling and huffing and puffing, he reached the highest branch. "Come here, little kitten," Papa called gently, and he tucked her under his sweater.

Then, sitting far out on a limb, Papa called, "Ah, how beautiful is God's creation! From here I can see all the way to Minsk!"

"What can you see?" the children asked.

"Apples, my children! Your papa sees apples, red and round, hiding their glory under the snow!"

"Apples?" gasped Mama. "Apples still on the tree? A miracle is happening here!"

"Apples are *always* a miracle," declared Papa as he joyfully tossed them down.

Quickly, they all rushed back inside their warm house. Mama and Papa peeled the apples and potatoes. And in the oil she had wisely saved just for Hanukkah, Mama fried so many latkes, they were heaped up high – a golden treasure!

Before the family sat down to eat, they sang a joyful song as they gazed at the final Hanukkah candles.

"Papa," Ezra said, "I have decided to name our dog Latke, because he found our potatoes."

"A wise choice, indeed," said Papa, smiling. "The name fits like a glove."

"And our cat's name is Applesauce!" said Rebecca.

"Because she found the apples! A perfect name!" said Mama.

Then Mama and Papa and Rebecca and Ezra and Latke and Applesauce ate latkes and applesauce — as much as their bellies could hold.

Now, was this a miracle? Who can say? It happened, and that is miracle enough for anyone!

The Holiday of Hanukkah

Like the Menashe family, Jewish people everywhere are always eager to celebrate Hanukkah. Why? Because it's such a happy holiday. Here is how the Hanukkah holiday began:

Over two thousand years ago, the Jewish people lived in a land called Judea (now called Israel). The center for their worship was the great Temple in the city of Jerusalem. And in the Temple, was the great menorah. Its light, which burned both day and night, was a brilliant symbol of holiness.

But a cruel king named Antiochus, who ruled the land of Judea, tried to force the Jews to worship his god, Zeus, instead of their own. When the Jews refused, the king sent his soldiers into the Temple, where they destroyed the holy books and desecrated holy objects, including the precious menorah.

But this tragedy didn't stop the Jewish people from worshipping God. And with great faith and courage, a man named Judah Maccabee led a small band of Jews who began to fight the king's army—an army which included thousands of soldiers and horsemen, and even some elephants!

After three years of struggle, the king's army gave up the fight— surely a miraculous victory!

After this great triumph, the Jewish people hurried to reclaim the great Temple. They cleaned it thoroughly, rebuilt the altar, and made a new menorah. Finally, it came time to rededicate the Temple to God. (The word "Hanukkah" means "dedication.")

But when they searched for oil to relight the giant menorah, they found only one small container of purified oil—just enough to last one day. But that oil burned on and on, day after day. In fact, it burned for *eight* days! Seeing this as a sign from God, Judah Maccabee declared, "Let these events be celebrated with mirth and gladness for all time to come!"

And that is exactly what the Jewish people do. Every year, in countries all around the world, families and friends gather to light candles and to feast for eight straight days! You may ask how latkes come into this story. Well, latkes are fried in oil, and that helps to remind us of the little jar of oil that burned miraculously for eight days!

Potato Latkes

6 medium-sized raw potatoes

1 large raw carrot

1 raw onion

1/4 cup matzo meal

2 raw eggs

1/4 cup salad oil

salt and pepper to taste

Grate and mix everything together. Have a grown-up help you fry large spoonfuls of the mixture in hot oil until golden brown. Serve with applesauce. (This latke recipe is a more elaborate version than the Menashes' simple one.)

How to play dreidel

To begin the game, all players get 10–15 objects (nuts, raisins, pennies, etc.). Everyone puts one object in "the pot" (the middle). Each player takes a turn spinning. Here is what each Hebrew letter on the side of the dreidel stands for:

נ (N) or nun stands for *nisht* or "nothing." If your dreidel lands on nun, do nothing.

ג (G) or gimel stands for *ganz* or "all." If your dreidel lands on gimel, take everything in the pot.

ה (H) or hay stands for *halb* or "half." If you get hay, take half of what's in the pot (plus one, if there's an odd number left).

ש (SH) or shin stands for *shtel* or "put in." If you get shin, put two objects into the pot. When only one object or none is left in the pot, every player adds one. When one person has everything, he or she wins!

And here is one explanation as to why we play with dreidels during Hanukkah: Although the cruel king Antiochus forbade Jews to study their Torah, the Jewish Bible, young boys would gather to study it secretly. And whenever they heard soldiers' footsteps coming, they'd take out their spinning tops and pretend that they were playing.

Today, boys and girls still spin the dreidel. The four letters written on its sides have a double meaning. The letters also stand for, *Nes Gadol Haya Sham,* or "A great miracle happened there." And it certainly did!

Other Books About Hanukkah

Chaikin, Miriam, (illus. Demi) *Light Another Candle: The Story and Meaning of Hanukkah*, Clarion Books/Ticknor and Fields, 1981.

Ehrlich, Amy, (illus. Ori Sherman) *The Story of Hanukkah*, Dial, 1989.

Kimmel, Eric A., (illus. Trina Schart Hyman) *Hershel and the Hanukkah Goblins*, Holiday House, 1989.